The mouse and the moon.

Words and pictures by
Ben Mowlah.

In a jungle wild, there lived a mouse,
whose lifelong dream was to leave his house.
To touch the moon was his greatest wish,
and make his mark on history with this.

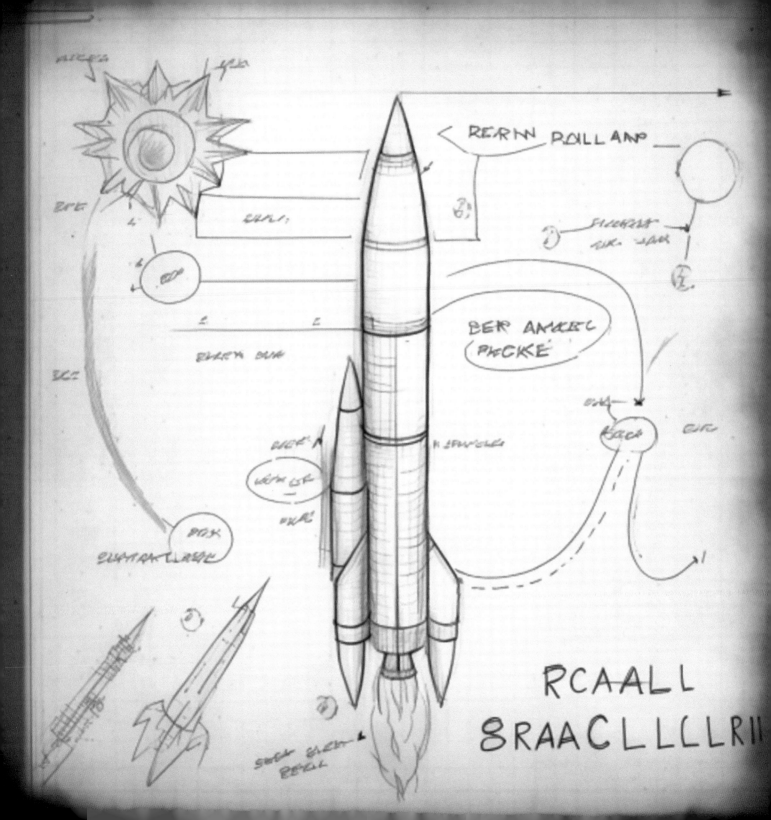

The mouse hatched a plan so daring and bold,
to build a rocket with his own hands to hold.
He gathered the tools and materials he'd need,
to make his dream a reality indeed.

To the wise tiger the mouse went for guidance,
on building a rocket that could brave the distance.
The tiger taught the mouse to face his fears,
and that bravery - not size - was what endears.

The strong elephant with his powerful might,
shared with the mouse the secrets of flight.
To build a rocket that could reach the moon,
strength and resilience it must imbue.

The inventive monkey with his clever mind,
showed the mouse what he needed to find.
To build a rocket that could soar to the skies,
imagination and innovation would arise.

The mouse sought the hippo with his sturdy frame,
to ask about protection and how to remain.
Safe from dangers the journey may bring,
a rocket to defend against anything.

The mouse worked hard with his team in tow,
to build a rocket that could withstand the blow.
From the jungle floor it rose to the sky,
the rocket was ready - the time was nigh.

Through the vast expanse of starry space,
the mouse and his rocket set their pace.
They sailed through the unknown in awe and delight,
through shooting stars and comets they took flight.

The mouse landed on the moon, so barren and cold,
his dream had come true - as he'd foretold.
He gazed about so far and below,
feeling grateful for his journey's flow.

The mouse asked the stars what he could see,
they replied "It's the Earth", shining with glee.
He realized that beauty can be seen from afar,
for the earth was as stunning as the moon by far.

The mouse looked around at the jungle he knew,
with newfound appreciation - a different view.
The trees, the flowers, the creatures that roam,
all held a beauty that he'd never before known.

As he settled back into his cozy home,
the mouse realized he needn't have flown.
For all the treasures that he sought,
were right here in the jungle all along, he thought.

The love of his friends and the warmth of the sun,
the joy of the wind and the rivers that run.
The moon may have been a dream come true,
but the real treasure was the life he already knew.

He had been so focused on his grand quest,
that he almost forgot what he possessed.
He learned a lesson he would never forget,
to cherish what he had and never regret.

Printed in Great Britain
by Amazon

29420665R00018